Learning to Love Him by Trusting Him

Book Study Guide

A Companion Guide for Reflection, Conversation and Growth

CE'CE PEREZ

First published by Writer's Wisdom a division of IBA Digital LLC 2025

This study guide is a nonfiction companion resource designed for personal refection, group of discussion, ministry use, and guised study. It is intended to be used alongside Learning to Love Him by Trusting Him. Any resemblance to actual persons or events in reflective examples is coincidental or used illustratively.

First Edition

ISBN: 979-8-9993619-2-9

For those who taught me love,

for the seasons that taught me to trust God,

and for every heart brave enough to change when
truth arrives,

This journey is ours together.

Table of Contents

Introduction

When I wrote **Learning to Love Him by Trusting Him**, my goal wasn't just to share lessons or stories. I wanted to invite you into places I've experienced and learned from—places we don't often talk about. I hoped to bring up truths we avoid and feelings that are hard to put into words.

As you read this book, I encourage you to meet your true self, explore who you are, and openly face what many of us have avoided. It means we pay attention to our real feelings, see who we are within, and understand what is deep inside our hearts and minds.

Each module invites us all to explore different aspects of love and self-growth. Module 1 helps us examine who we really are, our roles, strengths, smiles, and even the occasions we say, '*I'm fine.*' Later modules explore the fears we hold, the habits we keep, the walls we build, and the control we try to maintain. Each one helps us find the courage to break old patterns.

This process isn't about how things look. It's about being honest and letting God meet us in that truth.

We won't find repeated chapters.

We'll find opportunities to reflect, read scripture, and answer reflective questions, with room to be honest rather than aiming for perfect answers.

Some parts of this guide may feel sensitive. It's normal to have strong emotions during self-reflection. We should be gentle with ourselves—being vulnerable is a natural part of growing and healing.

Stretch us.

It might feel like someone finally put into words what we've felt for years.

That's okay. Growth doesn't usually wait for permission.

This guide walks **with** us, not ahead of us. Whether we're reading alone, with a group, with our spouse or partner, or trying to understand our own heart, let this be a gentle space to be real.

Bring a journal.

Bring our whole selves.

Perfection isn't invited or required.

I hope that as we read these pages, we'll recognize not just how we've loved before, but also how God is calling us to love now:

more open, grounded in truth, free, and whole.

Welcome to this journey, the work ahead, and the healing we may not have realized we needed.

Ready? Let's go.

Ce'ce

How to Use This Guide

This study guide delves deeper into **"Learning to Love Him by Trusting Him."** Encouraging honest reflection, conversation, and growth opportunities that can help in several ways: personal study, book clubs, small groups, couples, mentoring, or counseling. For example, a small group might meet weekly to talk about each module and share encouragement.

Couples might also use the guide during their devotional time, read lessons, and discuss their thoughts and feelings. Larger groups, such as church groups, marriage ministries, and men's or women's groups, can use the guide for small-group discussions before coming together as a whole. Groups from different backgrounds can adjust the guide to fit their experiences so everyone is included.

There's no set pace for this material. Healing doesn't happen on a schedule.

How to Work Through Each Module

Read the corresponding lessons in the book.

Notice what stands out or stays, especially what we feel, not just what we think.

Read the matching module in this guide.

Each module highlights a theme and invites us to look underneath the surface of patterns, habits, fears, and expectations about love and trust.

Engage the reflection questions.

These are not "test questions." They are invitations to be honest with ourselves and, if applicable, with our group or spouse.

Journal your responses

Use the margins or a separate notebook. Write freely. Pray on paper. Let thoughts come unedited.

Move at your own pace.

Most groups go through **one module per session**, usually in **60 to 90 minutes**, depending on how deep the discussion goes and what the group needs.

This guide isn't designed to rush through. If the conversation is honest and the work is progressing, **it's okay to slow down, pause, and finish the module in the next session.**

Use the time as a guide, not a strict rule. The goal isn't to finish every section quickly, but to take our time and let the lessons sink in.

Expect emotions, not perfection.

Some of us may feel encouraged, exposed, comforted, convicted, or relieved. It's normal.

This guide works well for:

- Women's or men's ministry groups
- Couples' groups
- Book clubs
- Mentoring relationships
- Counseling support

Suggested flow:

- Open with prayer or take a brief moment of silence.
- Read the assigned book lessons.
- Read the module aloud or silently.
- Discuss reflection questions
- Allow silence when emotions surface.
- Close with encouragement, not pressure.

Group agreements that help:

- Confidentiality is honored
- Sharing is optional
- Advice is limited; listening is priceless.
- No one is fixed or rushed.
- Respect different journeys and timelines.
- Boundary-Setting Checklist for Group Norms:
1. Establish confidentiality: *"What's shared here stays here."*

2. Emphasize that sharing is optional: "*Each person decides what to share.*"
3. Limit advice, prioritize listening: "*We are here to support, not solve.*"
4. Avoid rushing: "Honor the pace of each individual."
5. Acknowledge individual journeys: "*Appreciate diverse experiences and timelines.*"

A Note for Couples

Couples may choose to:

- Read separately, then discuss
- Read together and pause at questions.
- Journal privately and share only what feels safe.

The goal is not to "win" or diagnose each other—it is to understand the heart.

A Final Word Before Beginning

This guide is not asking us to be perfect.

It is inviting us to be **honest, present, and willing to grow**.

God meets us in truth.

He is gentle and patient with our process.

What You'll Need

To get the most out of this journey, it helps to have:

- Your copy of *Learning to Love Him by Trusting Him*
- this study guide
- a journal or notebook
- a pen or highlighter
- a Bible (digital or print)
- a quiet space or consistent meeting place
- an open mind, heart, and a willingness to be transparent with yourself

Optional but helpful:

- tissues (for the real moments)
- a trusted friend, spouse, mentor, or group to discuss reflections with

Perfection isn't a requirement to get started.

All that's needed is for us to show up.

Facilitator Guidelines

(For Groups, Retreats, and Counseling Settings)

This guide is meant to promote honest conversation, spiritual reflection, and real growth—not pressure or performance. As a facilitator, your job is to create a safe space where people can learn, speak, and heal at their own pace. You don't need special training to lead well; you just need to care and be willing to support others. Connecting with other facilitators and exchanging experiences and ideas can help everyone feel more confident as leaders.

1) *If someone becomes overwhelmed or withdrawn*

Emotional topics can come up unexpectedly, especially in mixed groups or for people carrying private pain.

If a group member becomes overwhelmed:

- Pause the moment without spotlighting them or putting them on display.
- Offer a gentle option: *"Let's take a breath together."*
- Give them permission to step out briefly or sit quietly without explanation.

- Keep our tone composed and steady. People feel more secure when the leader stays grounded.

If someone disengages:

- Don't call it out publicly.
- Continue without shaming or forcing participation.
- Check in privately afterward with care, not correction:
- *"I noticed today may have been heavy. Do you want to talk or just take your time?"*

Sometimes the most powerful facilitation is simply allowing space for people to process without being pushed.

2) *How to pace the group when people move at different speeds*

Every group has different processing styles. Some people speak quickly. Others need time to trust the room.

To keep pacing healthy:

- Focus on depth, not speed. Meaningful conversations matter more than finishing every question.
- Give time boundaries when needed: *"Let's spend five more minutes here, then we'll shift."*

- If a section sparks strong discussion, let the group stay with it, then assign the remaining questions for self-reflection.
- Use a finishing prompt to help transition:
- *"What's one takeaway you're carrying into the week?"*

We're not behind if the group is truly doing the work.

3) *When someone needs support beyond the group*

This group can be healing, but it isn't a replacement for professional care.

If someone needs deeper support:

- Encourage them to speak with a licensed counselor, pastor, or trusted professional.
- Offer resources if available through your church, ministry, or local community.
- If someone discloses serious emotional distress, give priority to safety and appropriate support outside the session.

A simple statement can help:

"You don't have to carry this alone, and you don't have to heal it only in this room."

4) Confidentiality and emotional safety (especially in new or mixed groups)

For the group to work, people must feel protected.

Before beginning each module, establish a basic agreement:

What's shared here stays here.

- People may share what they learned—but not who said it.
- No shaming, blaming, preaching at others, or "fixing" someone's story.
- No one is required to share details they aren't ready to reveal.
- Respect each other's pace, privacy, and process.

Say it plainly:

"We're here to grow, not perform. Honor the room."

5) Turning lessons into real change

Insight is powerful, but transformation happens when it becomes practice.

Explore the lessons together:

What might this look like in a real argument?

- *How could this change your tone at home?*

- *What opportunities are there for apologies, adjustments, or dealing with specific issues?*

Examples of everyday applications may include:

- Slowing down before reacting.
- Naming what's happening instead of shutting down.
- Asking for clarity instead of assuming the worst.
- Creating boundaries that limit outside influences and emotional access.
- Making space for reconnection after conflict, rather than staying cold.

Growth isn't about being perfect. It's about building new habits, one decision at a time.

Facilitator Tips

This section is highly valuable if the guide is used:

- in churches
- in counseling settings
- in book clubs
- by group leaders who may not be "teachers" but want guidance

Facilitator Tips

This study is about honest reflection, not perfection. If we're leading a group, our role isn't to fix people; it's to create a safe place for truth.

Helpful reminders as you lead:

- Begin each session by **setting the atmosphere**, not by lecturing. A calm, *'we're in this together'* attitude helps.
- Assess the environment. If emotions rise, slow down rather than push through material.
- Silence isn't failure. Sometimes, being quiet could mean people are thinking things through.
- Encourage reflection over debate. Each person's story is different.
- Don't force anyone to share. Voluntary sharing creates trust; pressure shuts it down.

- Protect confidentiality. What's shared should stay within the group.
- Model honesty. When we're real, others feel permission to be real too.
- Stay focused on self-reflection rather than diagnosing partners or spouses.
- End every session with hope, not with heaviness.

Our job isn't to have all the answers.

Our job is to hold space for growth.

Reader & Group FAQ

Logistics · How long should each module or session typically take?

Most groups do best with 60 to 90 **minutes per module**, depending on how much discussion unfolds.

A simple flow looks like this:

- **5–10 minutes**: welcome + check-in
- **20–30 minutes**: read the module + sit with it
- **25–40 minutes**: discussion + questions
- **5–10 minutes**: closing takeaway + prayer (optional)

If the conversation goes deeper than expected, it's okay to take a breath and pick up next time. This guide isn't about speed; it's about real life.

So if something hits you mid-session and you feel yourself shutting down, getting emotional, or wanting to retreat, that's not a problem. That's the work showing up.

We should give ourselves permission to pause, breathe, and take space if we need it. We shouldn't have to push through to prove we're strong.

If it feels intense, pause. That moment doesn't mean we're weak—it usually means something tender got touched.

We're allowed to:

- Take a breath and regroup
- Step out for a moment if you need to
- write instead of speak
- Skip a question that feels too exposed right now.
- Revisit the section later in private.

We don't have to share everything out loud to be doing real work.

Facilitation · Are there specific tips for first-time group leaders or facilitators?

Yes, and the most important one is simple: you don't have to be perfect to lead well. You just need to be steady.

Helpful reminders for facilitators:

- protect the room's atmosphere
- don't rush people through silence
- don't preach; guide the conversation
- don't try to "fix" someone's pain on the spot
- keep the group focused, but not pressured

A good facilitator doesn't take over the room. A good facilitator protects the space.

Privacy · How is confidentiality maintained in mixed or new groups?

Start every session with a clear agreement:

- What's shared here stays here.
- People can share what they learned, but **not who said what**.
- No repeating someone else's story outside the group.
- No shaming, mocking, or using vulnerability as ammunition later.
- No one is required to share details to participate fully.

This guide works best when the room feels emotionally safe, not exposed.

Participation · Is it okay to skip questions or modules that feel too sensitive right now?

Yes. This guide is meant to challenge you, not harm you.

If something is too sensitive right now, you can:

- Skip the question and keep going.
- Answer it privately instead of out loud.
- return to it later
- Simply write: "Not yet."

Growth doesn't require pressure. It requires willingness.

Module 1

The Love Script You Didn't Know You Had

Lessons 1–3

Love doesn't start when we're adults. It begins much earlier, when we were children watching the adults around us—our parents, aunties, and others—listening to conversations in the house and noticing silent signals. Before we met anyone, we were already forming our idea of love.

Those first pictures matter.

Some of us learn love through apology and repair.

Others learn it through silence, distance, fear, or control.

We learn to cling or disappear.

When we enter our first relationships, our hearts already carry ready-made scripts. Nobody formally hands them to us; they form slowly through experience. We do not walk in as blank slates. We walk in already shaped.

Lessons 1–3 invite us to look at that honestly. Not dramatically. Not emotionally. Just honestly.

Many of us don't fall in love with the person we're dating first. We fall in love with the idea of what love might fix: being chosen, being seen, or being rescued from loneliness or old hurt. When the relationship can't carry that weight, disappointment appears. It's not always because the person fails, but because the expectation is too much for anyone to hold.

Real love is nothing like fantasy. Fantasy agrees with us. Real love grows us. It shows us impatience we didn't notice before. It shows where we reach for control. It shows when we expect a partner to heal something we never brought to God. That awareness is not punishment. It is clarity.

Scripture describes love using practical words: patient, kind, truthful, steady. Not dramatic. Not perfect. Love is work, presence, listening, humility, and honesty. Real love requires participation, not rescue.

These scriptures also point toward trust — not casually, as in "I *trust God*" said in conversation — but the kind that asks something of us. Trust that God knows what He is doing in our story. Trust that His version of love sometimes interrupts our fantasies. Trust that His picking us matters more than those who did or didn't choose us.

The invitation here is simple and honest: none of us walks into love as a blank slate.

We bring history, habits, fears, and expectations, whether we mean to or not. We don't just bring feelings into love.

We bring history.

Beliefs we absorbed without realizing it.

Wishes that formed in lonely seasons.

Fears that still shake us and cause us to flinch when we know something feels off.

And expectations built from childhood: what we watched, what we lived through, what we never got, and what we promised ourselves we'd never repeat.

Add in the imagined endings—the version of love that was supposed to rescue us, finally make us feel chosen, finally make life feel safe—and it becomes clear:

Love doesn't start when we meet our partner.

Love starts in what shaped us long before them.

So we slow down here. Not to be dramatic. Just to be honest.

What early picture of love influenced me the most?

What did love seem to "mean" in the home I grew up in?

What did I quietly believe love would fix for me?

What am I still expecting my partner to heal that God may be calling me to face?

- What did I expect love to fix for me?
- Where do my expectations come from — experience, imagination, or fear?
- How does God's definition of love challenge mine today?

Our answers do not need decoration. They do not need church language or perfect wording. They need truth.

We are not rewriting our past. We're acknowledging its influence, so that it will stop steering our future.

Module 2

Baggage That Looks Like *"Normal"*

Lessons 4-6

No one steps into love empty-handed. Even the most capable, faith-filled people bring something with them. It's not always obvious or dramatic, but it's there.

Much of what shows up in us comes from experiences we never fully processed. Unacknowledged disappointments settle in quietly. Rejection changes how we enter rooms, how guarded we are, and how much of ourselves we let others see. Silence feels normal when speaking up isn't safe. Independence grows when relying on others is never felt possible. Over time, these experiences stop looking like wounds and start blending in as *'that's just me.'*

By the time connection enters the picture, life has already left fingerprints—losses we didn't finish grieving, disappointments we never processed, expectations that never got answered, and seasons where we had to grow up faster than we should've.

That doesn't go away just because we finally meet someone good.

It just shows up differently.

It hides under competence.

Under being "the strong one."

Under the smile that convinces everybody else we're fine.

And then, the moment love asks for softness... All that old weight starts talking.

Lessons 4–6 slow us down long enough to notice what we're carrying into love, not just what we say we've healed.

What shaped us doesn't always show up as heartbreak. It appears in overworking and staying strong, so no one sees the strain. It shows up in quick reactions because our nervous system is tired of surprises. It's there when we shut down or when emotions build up, because silence once kept things from getting worse. These aren't character flaws—they're ways we adapted.

Scripture tells us God stays close to the brokenhearted, not just those who seem strong, but those who stop pretending nothing is wrong. This closeness isn't pity; it's presence. God sees every moment when holding ourselves together feels like our only choice.

Love has a way of touching places in us we didn't realize were still tender.

Not in some dramatic, movie-scene way either.

In real life.

A short reply sounds cold.

A delayed response feels like rejection.

A change in tone feels like an attitude shift.

A small moment makes something significant rise up inside us—and we're not even sure why.

That's when we realize the reaction isn't only about what just happened.

It's about what that moment reminds us of.

It's about an old disappointment we never named.

Old hurts we learned to swallow.

Old fear that says, *"Here we go again.* According to sfhelp.org, relationship problems often stem from underlying issues that may not be directly caused by the person we love, but they can be the ones closest to us when these wounds are triggered. This is where Lessons 4 to 6 help bring greater understanding.

They help us separate the moment from the memory, so we stop taking out old pain on our partner. Relationships show us what we haven't processed—not to shame us, but to bring honesty to what still needs care. Love doesn't create these wounds. It reveals them.

Many of us describe our emotional residue as *"that's just who I am."* But it isn't our identity. It's an accumulation of things. It comes from seasons where the load exceeded capacity, and no one helped us carry it.

Guarding the heart is wise. Sealing it off entirely is survival. But intimacy cannot grow where access meets denial. When protection becomes permanent, closeness begins to feel threatening instead of nourishing.

This part of the work is not about blaming the past. It is about recognizing what follows us forward. Love struggles when yesterday keeps interrupting today—not because love is weak, but because unexamined patterns compete for space.

Lessons 4–6 slow us down long enough to notice when history is speaking through us.

Sit with these questions honestly:

- What emotional residue have I normalized that still shapes how I love?
- When did closeness begin to feel risky instead of restorative?
- Which reactions belong to an earlier version of me?
- What am I guarding out of wisdom—and what am I guarding out of fear?

- If God truly meets me in tenderness, what truth have I avoided admitting?

The goal is not to release everything at once.

The goal is recognition.

When what shaped us gets named, love no longer has to fight for space in the same crowded places. And once we finally recognize what we've been living with, we get to decide what stays—and what no longer belongs in our hands.

Module 3

When *"Being Strong"* Starts Costing You

Lessons 7–9

Control rarely looks like control at first.

It looks like staying ready.

Staying responsible.

Staying on top of everything so nothing falls apart.

Lessons 7–9 pull us into that part of love most people don't talk about out loud: the way we stay on alert even when nothing is technically wrong.

The relationship can be stable. The day can be typical. The conversation can be calm and still, but something inside us stays tense. Even when everything seems fine, we may still feel on edge, waiting for something to go wrong.

That's control.

Control isn't always loud, bossy, or obvious. Most of the time, it shows up dressed like responsibility. It sounds like, *"Let me handle it."* It feels like staying ready, keeping the structure together, and making sure nobody has to carry what we learned to carry alone.

At first, it feels wise. Over time, it becomes expensive.

Because control rarely stops at managing circumstances. It expands. It starts managing conversations, timing, reactions, and outcomes. Love stops feeling like a partnership and begins feeling like a system—organized, functioning, and guarded. Order may exist, but intimacy struggles to breathe.

Lessons 7–9 don't come from our personality—they come from our reflexes.

The reflex to stay in control.

The reflex to stay ready.

The reflex to keep our hands on everything because letting go feels reckless.

They bring clarity to the part of us that says, *"If I don't hold this together, it won't stay together."*

And here's what makes it tricky: peace can show up… and we still don't relax.

Not because we don't want peace.

Because we don't trust it.

Peace feels unfamiliar when life trained us to stay alert. So even when things are calm, the mind stays on duty. The heart keeps watching the room. The body keeps bracing, as if something bad is about to happen next.

Lessons 7–9 expose that pattern so love can breathe—and so trust can stop being something we talk about and start being something we live.

The issue isn't that we don't want calm—it's that calm feels unfamiliar when chaos once felt normal. So when love shows up steady—patient, consistent, safe—part of us stays suspicious anyway. We don't know what to do with someone who doesn't make us beg. We don't know how to settle into a relationship that doesn't demand constant monitoring. The hand still reaches for the steering wheel, because letting go feels like a risk.

And surrender may feel like losing.

But surrender, absolute surrender, doesn't mean we become invisible. It doesn't mean silencing ourselves or putting up with things we shouldn't. It means letting go of what God never asked us to carry. It's the heart finally admitting, *"I can't keep running this whole thing."*

Stillness sounds simple until you've spent your life believing that being still means being vulnerable. This kind of stillness takes trust, faith, and strength—not the kind that comes from holding everything together, but from believing God can handle it.

Lessons 7–9 also confront what we've been calling "*help.*" Helping can be love, or it can be control with a softer name. The difference shows up in the atmosphere. When control leads, pressure rises. Not always conflict—but pressure. Pressure to do it right. Pressure to perform. Pressure to explain. Pressure to maintain peace at any cost, because relaxing feels irresponsible.

That isn't love's assignment.

Love is not supposed to feel like something we have to manage to survive.

This section also introduces the right way to submit before anyone can twist it. Scripture doesn't teach submission as dominance, silence, or a power grab. It teaches mutual humility and shared honor. It teaches a posture that says, "*We are not enemies. We are not competing. We are building under God.*"

In that kind of submission, nobody loses. What wins is peace. What wins is truth. What wins is unity. What wins is God's order—because when God leads the relationship, fear doesn't have to.

Lessons 7–9 aren't asking us to trust without question. They're calling us to trust God deeply enough to stop letting fear make decisions, confusing control with wisdom, or calling anxiety "*discernment.*"

Control can prevent collapse, but it can also prevent closeness.

So sit with these questions and answer them honestly, without polishing or performing:

- Where do I reach for control first—my tone, my silence, my assumptions, or my need to *"handle it"*?
- What am I afraid will happen if I stop managing everything?
- What does *"being still"* feel like to me—peaceful or unsafe? Why?
- Do I treat my partner like a teammate... or like someone I have to supervise to feel secure?
- Where do I call anxiety *"wisdom"* because it feels easier than admitting fear?
- What would it look like to trust God with the outcome instead of trying to control the process?

They show what happens when caring turns into holding on too tightly, when love starts to feel like a job we can't leave. Control may keep things from falling apart, but it also keeps things from feeling free.

And love can't fully breathe where we manage everything else.

Module 4

Triggers, Voices, and Real Life

Lessons 10–12

Love changes when it stops living in our heads and starts living in our hearts.

Not because love is weak—but because real life is demanding.

Real life comes with routines that don't pause for romance, stress that doesn't care how much we prayed, and a tiredness that makes simple conversation feel like work.

Lessons 10–12 focus on the place where love isn't just a feeling anymore. It becomes a choice we make when we're hungry, busy, irritated, distracted, or tired.

The question shows up, and we hate admitting:

Why does this feel harder than I thought it would?

It isn't always doubt.

Often, its growth demands our attention.

Love doesn't erase what shaped us. It brings it to the surface. It reveals how we respond when plans fall apart, when we feel overlooked, when effort feels uneven, or when closeness feels good but also exposes something tender.

This part of the book points to a truth we can't dress up or hide:

Two people can love each other deeply and still have emotional gaps that keep turning into friction.

Not because either of us is malicious—but because habits don't disappear. They show up inside commitment.

Lessons 10–12 turn our attention to what's happening beneath the words—the assumptions we form, the stories we tell ourselves, and the conclusions we reach without evidence. Conflict begins quietly here, not with shouting, but with interpretation.

A small moment lands, and the mind fills in the blanks:

"They don't care."

"I'm on my own again."

"Here we go."

"I knew this wouldn't last."

Once those thoughts take over, we stop responding to what's happening and start reacting to a past that still has influence.

That's why these lessons matter.

They don't teach us how to avoid tension—they teach us how to keep tension from ruining the relationship.

Here is where intimacy matures.

Not just physical closeness, though our bodies always respond to the emotional climate, but intimacy as safety. Connection. The ability to say what's real without turning it into a fight. The ability to be honest without being harsh, to ask for clarity without accusing, and to admit, *"I'm not okay,"* without making it a punishment.

Guessing gets expensive.

It costs peace, trust, and softness.

The truth is, both partners may be trying and still miss each other.

Lessons 10–12 invite a different kind of awareness. Not self-criticism, but honesty. Honesty about spiraling, assuming, guarding, or holding our partner responsible for pain they didn't cause.

It isn't weakness, but emotional maturity showing up in real time.

So we pause and sit with it, no performing, no pretending, just truth:

- Where do I interpret instead of communicate?

- When love feels off, do I move toward clarity or distance?
- What story starts running when I feel unseen or unsure?
- Where do I expect my partner to read my mind, rather than letting my needs have a voice?
- What would change if I chose honesty early instead of waiting until I'm emotionally loaded?

Lessons 10–12 aren't here to shame us. They interrupt the cycle.

Love doesn't break most relationships.

Unspoken assumptions do.

Unaddressed patterns do.

Fear disguised as *"I'm fine"* does.

And none of this is permanent.

It simply requires a decision—to stay aware, stay present, and stop letting old reflexes drown out the love we're building.

Module 5

Staying Present When It's Easier to Retreat

Lessons 13–15

Love doesn't stay cute forever.

It may start that way, full of intention, hope, and the thought, *"we'll never be like them."* But Lessons 13–15 take us into the part of love that doesn't care about our speeches. It's where real life puts pressure, and the heart shows what it really trusts.

It's about courage. Not the kind we clap for, but that shows up when our emotions get thick, when comfort disappears, when it feels easier to shut down, shift blame, get sarcastic, or go cold so we can feel like we're in control. This courage is crucial because it lays the groundwork for long-term relationship health, helping to build resilience and trust over time.

Truthfully, fear doesn't always look like panic.

It can sound like an attitude or hide behind *"I'm fine."*

It shows up as a distance that looks mature but feels like punishment.

It turns a simple conversation into a standoff where nobody wants to admit what they need.

Lessons 13–15 don't let that behavior hide behind personality.

They call it what it is: a response, a learned reflex, a way of staying protected without having to admit, "*I feel exposed right now.*"

Courage looks like staying in the room anyway.

Not to argue better, but to love better.

It means carefully choosing words when the tongue wants to cut, or saying what's real without making it sound violent. It means not turning honesty into a weapon, not turning silence into power, and not forcing our partner to guess what's wrong with us while acting like everything is okay.

This is where things get uncomfortable, because it challenges our pride.

Pride won't want to soften at first. It doesn't want to admit hurt, but would rather stay misunderstood than vulnerable; would rather act unbothered than risk hearing, "*I didn't realize I was doing that.*"

Courage doesn't need control to feel safe.

It has enough strength to be honest without trying to win.

Joshua 1:9 means something deeper here. It's not just a motivational quote—it's a reminder that strength doesn't come from being fearless. It comes from staying connected to God even when we feel afraid. God isn't asking us to pretend we're not nervous about love. He's asking us to trust Him and keep going, even when we are.

These lessons also expose a truth most people won't admit: the challenging moments aren't always about what's happening right now, but about what the moment reminds us of: old disappointments, rejection, the versions of ourselves that had to survive. When that fear wakes up, it starts talking fast. It starts narrating the relationship. It starts assuming the worst and calling it discernment.

Relationships get tired.

Not because love isn't there.

Because fear keeps interrupting it.

Ephesians 3:16 speaks to the kind of strength this season requires—inner strength. The kind that doesn't need to dominate, control, or protect itself with sharp edges, that can say, *"I felt hurt,"* without following it with an attitude, can listen without preparing a comeback, or can own a mistake without adding a full explanation to make sure nobody thinks less of us.

It's what changes the atmosphere.

Not perfection, constant agreement, or pretending everything is okay.

But a willingness to stay honest, open, and present, even when emotions are intense.

So sit with these questions. Answer them plainly. No editing. No polishing.

- Where do I get the most defensive in love, and what am I afraid that means about me?
- What do I usually do when I feel emotionally exposed—do I soften, fight, shut down, or control the room?
- What truth have I been avoiding because it would require humility instead of pride?
- What does courage look like for me this week—in my tone, my honesty, my restraint, and my consistency?
- Where is God asking me to show up differently so love can feel safe again?

Lessons 13–15 aren't calling anyone weak.

They're calling us higher.

Because love doesn't just need feelings, it requires courage that stays.

Module 6

Peace, Pressure, and the Cost of Avoidance

Lessons 16–18

Desire doesn't fade because the love is gone.

It fades when tension goes unresolved, trust feels unstable, and closeness feels forced.

We don't always want to say this out loud because it feels so real. But love isn't just about feelings—it's about how we live. Intimacy grows or fades depending on the atmosphere we create.

A relationship can look stable on the outside, with responsibilities handled, life moving, and the family functioning, but still feel emotionally strained in private. Not because either partner has stopped caring, but because care isn't the same as connection. Love can exist while softness slowly fades.

Lessons 16–18 matter. They don't just address conflict; they address the atmosphere. They show us that intimacy can't stay free if the relationship feels heavy. Sex is rarely the first issue; it's often where the problem starts to show.

The body doesn't ignore emotional tension.

Desire doesn't thrive in pressure.

Closeness struggles when unresolved frustration keeps sitting between two partners like a third party.

It's not about blame. It's about honesty.

Love doesn't always walk out. Sometimes safety does.

And once safety is gone, the relationship can still look stable on paper but feel heavy in real life.

A partner can feel loved and still feel on edge—not because they want to leave, but because they don't know what version of the conversation they're about to get. So they keep it light. Keep it safe. Keep it on the surface.

And that's how intimacy starts thinning out.

Intimacy won't stay easy in that kind of atmosphere, because closeness needs space to grow.

Most of the time, repair doesn't begin in the bedroom. It starts with how we carry ourselves toward each other—how we speak when we're frustrated, how we handle disagreement, and whether respect survives correction.

Truth matters. But how we handle it matters just as much.

Avoiding hard conversations doesn't bring peace. It only delays problems or slowly makes the relationship feel cold.

Real love learns how to tell the truth without turning it into a weapon. It knows how to confront what's real while still honoring the person standing before us.

So take a moment and sit with this honestly:

- Where has tension gone unaddressed long enough that it's starting to affect closeness?
- Does intimacy feel safe, strained, distant, forced, avoided... or simply "*off*"?
- What emotional pattern keeps showing up before things shut down between us?
- When correction happens, does it sound like love... or like contempt?
- What does my partner experience from me lately—peace, pressure, criticism, or warmth?
- What needs to be repaired emotionally so intimacy stops carrying the weight it never should have?

These lessons don't end with shame. They end by taking responsibility.

Because love can survive a lot—but it thrives where it's protected, honored, and handled with care.

And what we handle with care has room to grow.

Module 7

Present but Emotionally Unavailable

Lessons 19-21

No one storms out. No one screams. But the room starts feeling colder anyway.

Life keeps moving. Responsibilities pile up, conversations continue, and routines stay the same. From the outside, everything still looks fine.

But something shifts.

It's not always visible, but it's real. The body stays present, but the heart steps back. Not out of coldness, but out of self-protection. Because showing up fully starts to cost more than it used to.

It doesn't begin with a blow-up. It starts when the same things keep happening, and explaining ourselves feels pointless. Not because we don't care. Because we're tired of caring out loud and still feeling unheard.

So you adjust.

Not with threats. Not with drama.

With distance.

Withdrawal isn't something we invent as adults. It's a survival pattern we learn early. Honesty creates tension. Emotions have consequences. Needing something is called "*too much*." So being quiet feels safer than speaking up. Distance feels easier than being vulnerable. Eventually, we start pulling back without even planning to, to keep steady.

Retreat doesn't happen because love is missing.

It happens because support feels inconsistent.

That's what makes it so dangerous. Nothing looks broken, but it just gets quieter inside. Conversations become flat. Warmth fades. Things stay polite. The relationship stays together, but something important starts to disappear: emotional closeness.

And God sees that shift long before anyone else does.

Psalm 34:18 reminds us that God stays close to the brokenhearted. Not to shame the retreat—He exposes it so it doesn't become permanent. He pulls us back toward honesty before distance becomes a way of life.

This section isn't about forcing vulnerability. It's about noticing when disconnection starts to settle in, while the relationship is still within reach.

The truth is, what lies beneath withdrawal is rarely complicated.

The heart wants reassurance without begging and understanding without defending. Safety without shrinking. And when it doesn't feel safe to ask, distance starts looking like the only option.

Staying present doesn't always require a long talk. Sometimes it starts with one honest sentence before silence takes over:

"That landed heavier than I expected."

"I need a minute before I shut down."

"I'm here... but I'm struggling."

Speaking the truth early keeps disconnection from taking root.

When withdrawal lasts too long, it starts to feel normal. The relationship stays together, but the warmth fades. Not because love was fake or anyone is bad, but because no one stops what's quietly coming apart.

So sit with these questions privately first. Answer them honestly—no cleanup needed:

- When do I notice myself pulling back even though I'm still physically present?
- What taught me that silence felt safer than honesty?
- What do I usually want in those moments but struggle to say?
- How does my partner experience me when I retreat?

- How do I want God to meet me when I feel myself closing off?

It isn't about doing more.

It's about staying open and reachable.

Because love can't stay healthy if the heart keeps slipping out of reach.

Module 8

The Bedroom Tells the Truth

Lessons 22-24

Lessons 22–24 don't focus on surface problems. They pull us into what happens when two people try to build something sacred, but outside voices and quiet wounds keep intruding on the relationship.

Outside influence doesn't always come in loudly. Most of the time, it slips in quietly.

It shows up through family opinions we didn't ask for but still carry.

Well-meaning friends speak up out of fear. Old attachments that haven't fully ended. "Helpful" conversations that leave one of us feeling irritated, insecure, or off balance. Even comparison—the kind that makes us doubt what we prayed for because we see another couple's life as effortless.

That kind of interference doesn't always destroy relationships.

But it does change the atmosphere inside it.

It breeds tension instead of peace.

It makes one of us feel monitored rather than valued.

It turns insignificant misunderstandings into emotional distance.

It teaches us to treat our private issues as if they were public discussions.

Before we know it, we're trying to build unity while letting outsiders have a say in our relationship.

That's why these lessons press on boundaries—not as control, but as protection.

A boundary isn't "cut off your family."

A boundary is "our relationship doesn't run on another person's emotions."

A boundary isn't isolation.

A boundary brings clarity.

Because unity can't grow where loyalty remains divided.

This part of the book forces us to answer an uncomfortable but necessary question:

Are we building a life together... or maintaining two separate worlds under one roof?

Unity isn't just a word we say at weddings or a lovely caption on social media. Unity shows up in real decisions: who has access to our private struggles, whose voice matters in our home, and whether the relationship feels like a partnership or a burden.

And when unity is shaky, intimacy usually pays the price.

Lesson 24 goes there—and not in a sugarcoated way.

Sex is rarely the first problem.

It's often where, for some of us, the problem shows up.

Relationships can look stable on the outside, with bills paid, kids raised, church attended, and responsibilities handled, but we can still feel emotionally disconnected in private. Disconnection doesn't just affect our conversations; it affects our closeness, affection, and how safe it feels to be desired, touched, pursued, or vulnerable.

We can feel loved and still feel guarded, stay faithful and still feel unseen, and share our home and still feel alone inside it.

Our bodies respond to the emotional climate of our relationship.

When the atmosphere gets heavy, intimacy suffers and carries a weight it shouldn't. It becomes strained rather than natural, tense rather than safe, and a duty rather than a connection.

That doesn't mean love is dead.

It means love needs repair.

And repair doesn't begin in the bedroom.

Repair begins in the atmosphere.

It begins with tone, honor, restraint, and with truth spoken without cruelty.

Relationships can survive disagreement, but they can't thrive under constant tension.

Love doesn't need perfection, but it does require care. These lessons aren't pushing us to perform; they're guiding us toward alignment with God, with truth, and with the kind of love that feels safe in private, not just impressive in public.

So take a moment and sit with these questions. Answer them honestly, without cleaning them up.

- What outside voices have more access to my relationship than they've earned?
- Where have I allowed "support" to become interference?
- What am I protecting in my relationship, and what am I exposing too freely?
- When my partner is with me, do they feel peace—or pressure?
- What has intimacy been like lately: safe, tense, distant, forced, avoided, or strained?
- What does unity look like in our day-to-day decisions—not just in our intentions?

- What needs to shift so closeness can feel natural again?

Lessons 22–24 don't end with shame. They end with an invitation.

Because love can survive a lot.

But love thrives where it's protected.

And what we protect has room to grow.

Conclusion

We've reached the end of the study guide, but not the end of the work.

What we've done here wasn't just about finishing pages. It was about starting something inside us that doesn't end when the book closes. We've named truths, faced feelings we usually avoid, and let God speak into places that have been quiet for a long time. That matters.

Now the focus shifts from reading to living.

This next part isn't about perfection or "doing everything right." It is about practicing what you discovered: noticing when old patterns reappear, speaking honestly rather than disappearing emotionally, letting love meet us where we are, inviting God into our reactions, not just our prayers, and choosing connection instead of control when fear rises. To make this a habit, consider a small weekly ritual, such as a 'three-minute gratitude exchange' every Sunday. This practice lets you share what you're grateful for and serves as a gentle reminder each week of the journey you're on.

- noticing when old patterns reappear
- speaking honestly instead of disappearing emotionally

- letting love meet us where we really are
- inviting God into our reactions, not just our prayers
- choosing connection instead of control when fear rises

Growth isn't measured by how loudly we change, but by the small choices we make on ordinary days: the tone we soften, the conversation we finish, the apology we mean, the boundary we respect, and the prayer we whisper instead of shutting down.

If we're doing that work, we're moving forward.

Here are some gentle next steps we may want to take:

Consider forming a follow-up group or scheduling regular check-ins with fellow participants to foster a supportive environment where you can share progress, offer encouragement, and sustain growth. Being part of a community that continues past this study can help reinforce what we've learned and keep us connected.

- Reread sections of the study or book that tugged at us.
- Journal the moments where we notice ourselves reacting differently.
- Invite our spouse, partner, or trusted friend into an honest conversation.
- Pray specifically about the themes that surfaced repeatedly for us. If you're not sure

how to begin, here are a few prayer prompts: "Help me release control, trusting in Your plan above my own." "Grant me the patience to listen and the courage to speak my truth with love." "Guide us in creating a home where peace and understanding thrive." "Show me how to embrace vulnerability as a strength, not a weakness." These prompts are meant to inspire us in our own words and to invite God into the specific areas we've journeyed through.

- Give ourselves credit for the progress we would usually overlook

And when we stumble, as we all do, remember this truth:

Stumbling doesn't erase growth.

Philippians 1:6 reminds us that the One who began this work will continue it. We are not carrying this alone. God is committed to our healing, even on days we feel tired of working on it.

I'm thankful that you let me walk beside you in this part of your story.

Thank you for choosing honesty over autopilot.

Thank you for believing your heart is worth the effort.

Move forward in your life gently but keep moving forward.

Your next chapter isn't waiting on perfection.

It's waiting on willingness.

Ce'ce

Continue the Journey

Learning to Love Him by Trusting Him

The companion book that explores the deeper emotional and spiritual journey behind the reflections in this guide. Through honest storytelling and faith-centered insight, it invites readers to look beneath patterns of fear, trust, and connection in relationships.

Scan to learn more or order the book.

writerswisdom.com

Coming Soon

Between Seasons

A forthcoming book by Ce'ce Perez exploring the quiet
in-between spaces of life—when relationships shift,
identities evolve, and faith must grow deeper than
certainty.

For anyone navigating the space between what was and
what comes next, *Between Seasons* offers reflection,
honesty, and hope.

Join the update list at
writerswisdom.com

Stay Connected

If this guide encouraged reflection or meaningful conversation in your life, I invite you to stay connected for future books, resources, and conversations about faith, growth, and relationships.

writerswisdom.com